The Mole's Daughter

An adaptation of a Korean folktale

Julia Gukova

Annick Press • Toronto • New York

A mole and his wife had raised the most beautiful daughter imaginable. She seemed perfect in every way. One day her father said to her mother,

"I can hardly imagine marrying her off to a mere mole. She is so exquisite, she must have the most highly respected, most powerful husband in the world. The sky is the limit."

When the daughter heard these words, she began to cry and said, "But my dear father, what would I do with the sky as a husband?" Alas, the proud father wouldn't listen, and she cried herself to sleep that night.

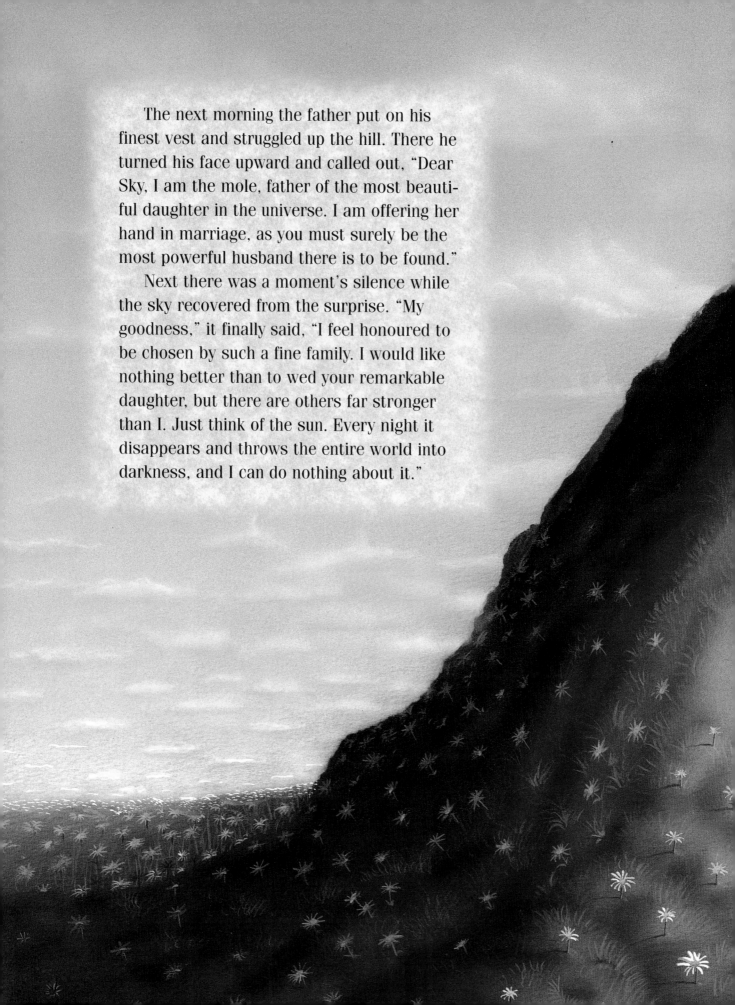

The next morning the father put on his finest vest and struggled up the hill. There he turned his face upward and called out, "Dear Sky, I am the mole, father of the most beautiful daughter in the universe. I am offering her hand in marriage, as you must surely be the most powerful husband there is to be found."

Next there was a moment's silence while the sky recovered from the surprise. "My goodness," it finally said, "I feel honoured to be chosen by such a fine family. I would like nothing better than to wed your remarkable daughter, but there are others far stronger than I. Just think of the sun. Every night it disappears and throws the entire world into darkness, and I can do nothing about it."

"Oh, dear," said Father Mole, "I had not given it any thought. Thank you for pointing it out." And he waited at home 'til the sun was high in the sky, then went out to the field.

"Dear Sun, Your Honour," began the mole, "I have come to tell you of a singular beauty, my daughter. She would make you a wonderful wife. And you, the most powerful, the strongest—" Before he could finish, the sun replied, "Dear Mole, how can I thank you for your trust in my strength? But you are mistaken to believe that I am the strongest in the sky. Consider the mighty cloud. It simply drifts in front of me at will, and my face is hidden, my light and heat diminished, sometimes for days. I can do nothing about it."

"Oh, dear," said Father Mole, "I had not given it any thought. Thank you for pointing it out." Shaking his head in confusion, the mole returned to the family home, where the daughter was still sobbing, comforted by the mother. But the father ignored them.

He went to look at the sky from time to time until he spotted a single cloud, floating gently along. As fast as he could move the mole made his way across the field and looked up. "O Cloud," he said, "how lovely you are, soft and delicate in appearance, yet large and powerful beyond description. Why, you can darken the land simply by moving in front of the great sun. Yet you seem lonely up there. Have you given any thought to the idea of matrimony? My daughter is the most beautiful creature in the whole wide world. She would make you a loving wife."

"Dear Mole, I'm honoured," said the cloud, "but if it's my power you find impressive, it is nothing compared to that of the wind. He is really the king. He just appears and blows, and I have to move along. I can do nothing about it. Speak to the wind."

And the mole did. No sooner had he begun than a fierce storm came up, driving more clouds and rain across the sky, so the mole had to shout to be heard. Clearly in awe of this powerful display, he repeated his offer. It took quite a while before the wind finished blowing and responded.

"My dear Mole," he said, slightly out of breath, "for one hundred years I have been trying to blow down that stone wall at the end of the field. It just stands there and resists me. The sun and rain have not been able to move it either. The wall is supreme!"

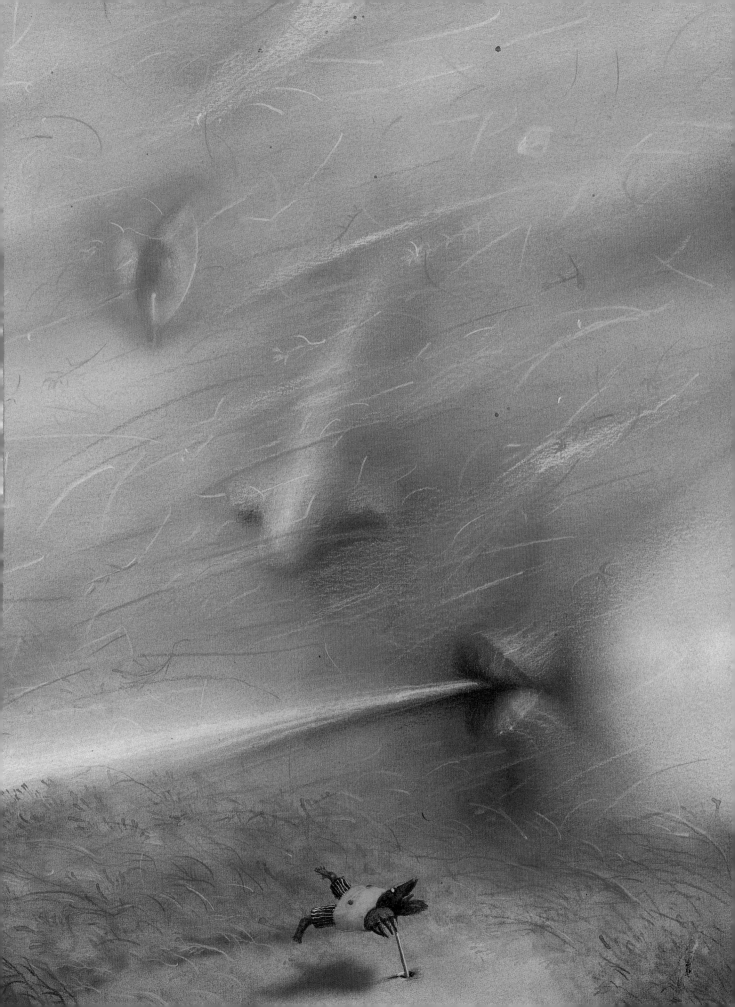

The mole was getting very discouraged. He returned home and told his wife and daughter what had happened. The daughter listened. Then she wiped away her tears and said, "Dear, beloved father. I know you just want what is best

for me, but you would not seriously think of
wedding me to an old dusty stone wall?"

Father Mole was finally growing sad to see
his daughter so unhappy. He said, "Well, let's at
least all go over and take a look at that wall."

And they went at once. There it was, a massive, ancient stone structure of awe-inspiring height and depth. No one said anything until, all of a sudden, they felt a familiar gentle scrabbling and heaving, and right in front of their eyes a molehill appeared and the most appealing young mole stuck out his head. He looked all around him and then spied Mr. Mole's daughter.

"Good morning, what a lovely meadow you have here! So *this* is what it looks like on this side of the wall."

But he had eyes only for the daughter, who had a radiant smile on her face.

She took aside her father and whispered, "If the sun, the rain and the fierce winds cannot overwhelm it, I can easily think of someone for whom this wall is no obstacle..."

"What are you talking about?" asked the father.

"The mole!" said the daughter. "He simply burrowed underground, as we do every day, and came up on the other side, whether the wall permitted it or not. I beg you, please let me marry a mole."

The mother had heard these last words, and she spoke up. "What an extraordinary daughter we have. She is not only beautiful, but wise as well. She will be a fine mole wife." And so it was done. The wedding was prepared...

...and the sky, the sun, the cloud, the wind, and even the wall were all invited to the party!

Many versions of this ancient folktale exist, ranging in country of origin from India through Southeast Asia and Japan to Siberia. Some feature rats or mice as the protagonists, and the natural elements approached by the proud father vary slightly. The version adapted by Annick Press is from Korea and the only one we found that featured a family of moles.

THE CANADA COUNCIL | LE CONSEIL DES ARTS
FOR THE ARTS | DU CANADA
SINCE 1957 | DEPUIS 1957

We acknowledge the support of the Canada Council for the Arts for our publishing program. We also thank the Ontario Arts Council.

Cataloguing in Publication Data

Gukova, Julia
  The mole's daughter

ISBN 1-55037-525-3 (bound) ISBN 1-55037-524-5 (pbk.)

1. Tales – Korea. 2. Moles (Animals) – Folklore. I. Title.

PZ8.1.G85Mo 1998   398.2'095190452027   C97-932264-2

The art in this book was rendered in mixed media.
The text was typeset in Fenice.

Distributed in Canada by:
Firefly Books Ltd.
3680 Victoria Park Avenue
Willowdale, ON
M2H 3K1

Published in the U.S.A. by Annick Press (U.S.) Ltd.
Distributed in the U.S.A. by:
Firefly Books (U.S.) Inc.
P.O. Box 1338
Ellicott Station
Buffalo, NY 14205

Printed and bound in Canada by
Friesens, Altona, Manitoba.